First published in the United States, Great Britain, Canada, Australia, and New Zealand in 2014
by NorthSouth Books, Inc., an imprint of NordSüd Verlag AG, CH-8005 Zürich, Switzerland.

Distributed in the United States by NorthSouth Books Inc., New York 10016.
Library of Congress Cataloging-in-Publication Data is available.
ISBN: 978-0-7358-4113-0
Printed in Germany by Offizin Andersen Nexö Leipzig GmbH, 04442 Zwenkau, August 2013.

1 3 5 7 9 • 10 8 6 4 2
www.northsouth.com

FSC
www.fsc.org
MIX
Paper from
responsible sources
FSC® C012425

Willy Puchner

The ABC of Fabulous Princesses

North South

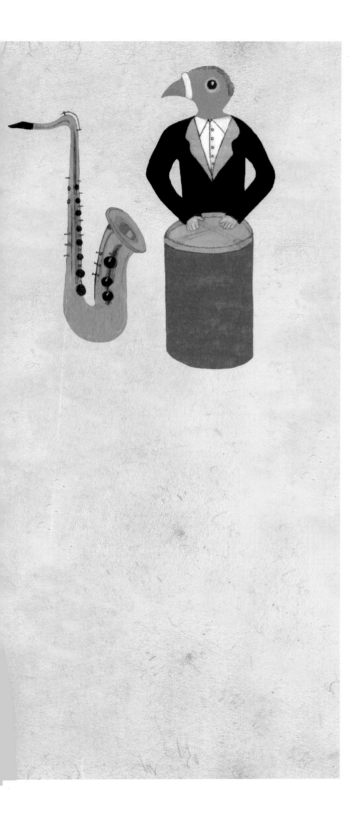

*P*rince William wishes to meet a wonderful princess to share his throne. While he is happy to play his drum and gaze out the window as he waits to meet just the right one, his family thinks it's time to weigh in. They've worked unwaveringly to woo princesses from around the world so that he (and you) can meet each of them.

*Twenty-six princesses!* Prince William is weary even thinking about it.

Won't you help him winnow the list and decide?

Princess Anna comes from Amsterdam.
She is adoring, ambitious, and athletic.
She loves apples, avocados, and almonds
with apricot sauce. She swims astonishing
distances, attracting an audience when
in Argentina. Anna brings an
ambrosia apple for Prince William.

Princess Beatriz comes from Bogotá. She is bashful, bright, and at times badly behaved. She likes bacon, blueberries, and banana bread. Beatriz is a bibliophile and spends her time reading best sellers while her beagle barks in the bookstore. She brings Prince William blueprints of the brilliant Baron Bluebeak and his band of brothers.

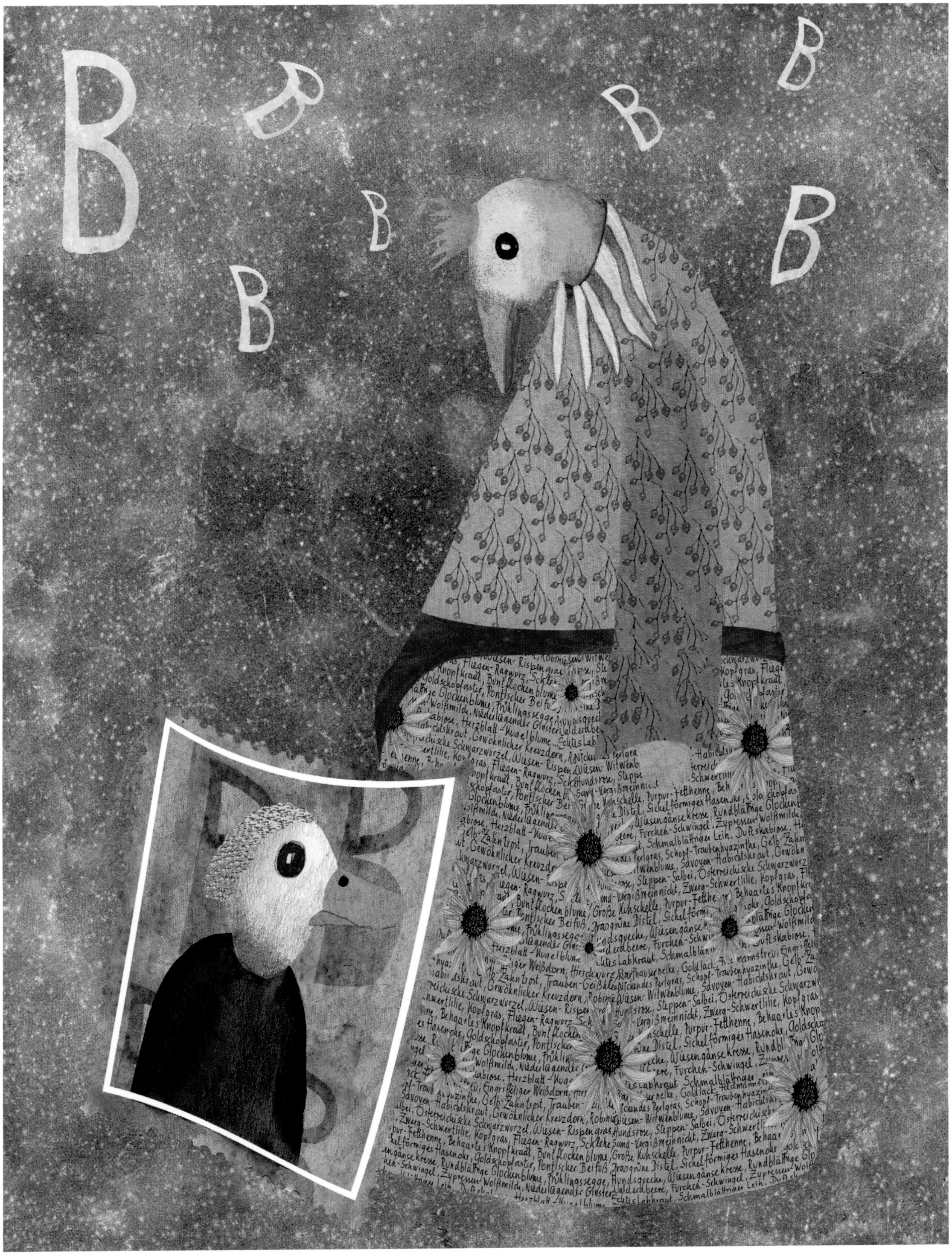
B
B
B
B
B
B
B
B

Princess Coletta comes from Caracas. She is clever, charming, and constantly chatty. She likes cheeseburgers, cheesecake, and cheese steak. Did she tell you she cherishes cheese? Although she's completely content with chocolate. She conjures things to create chimerical compositions and cares for cuckoos and, some years, cicadas. Coletta brings a cello from Chile for Prince William.

Princess Dagoberta comes from
Djibouti. She is daring, dramatic,
and a little dangerous. She likes
dumplings for dinner and dragon
fruit for dessert. She draws designs
with her daughters, Dolly, Dodo, and
Doro, and dares to dance with
desert dogs. Dagoberta brings
Prince William thirteen
dusty-rose dreamers.

Princess Elmira
comes from
Ethiopia.
She is extravagant,
empathetic, and
enormously emancipated.
She enjoys eating eel
with eggplant and endive.
She plays the English horn
and engages in exciting expeditions.
For Prince William, Elmira brings
a parade of eleven elegant elephants.

Princess Florentine lives in Finland.
She is foolish, funny, and forgetful.
She eats fish filets with fennel,
French fries, and fruit. She plays
the fipple flute on Fridays (when
she doesn't forget) and frolics with
flickering fireflies. Florence brings
Prince William a friendly frog.

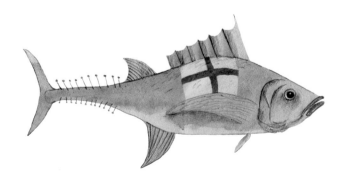

Princess Gala
comes from
Guatemala. She is
graceful, glamorous,
but sometimes
a little greedy.
She eats everything
with garlic and
ginger—goulash,
garbanzo beans,
and greens.
Gala loves gardening
and playing guitar.
For Prince William,
Gala brings a green
snake and a game
fowl, if she
agrees to
give them away.

Princess Holly
comes from Hawaii.
She is helpful, humorous,
and habitually happy.
She likes to eat hamburgers
and huckleberries
with honey.
She plays harmonica
and hums hymns.
Holly brings Prince William
a handsome harlequin.

Princess Indira comes from India.
She is intelligent, imaginative, and inquisitive.
She eats food from Italy, Indonesia,
Iceland, and, of course, India.
She interrogates inmates during
investigations and loves inclement weather
and iridescent rainbows.
She brings Prince William
irresistible Indian spices.

Princess Jolanda
comes from Johannesburg.
She is judicious, joyful, and,
on rare occasions, a bit juvenile.
She loves juice and jambalaya.
Jolanda sounds her Jaeger rifle to
jump-start her jamborees.
She brings Prince William
a jazzy horn and a big
jungle cat.

Princess Kalila
comes from Kuwait.
She is keen, kooky, and kind.
She likes to eat kebabs with
ketchup, kohlrabi, and kiwi.
She plays the kazoo and loves
to travel to Kenya, Korea,
and Katmandu.
Kalila brings Prince William
six kindly cranes.

Princess Lubaya
comes from Libya.
She is lovable, lazy,
and lucky.
She likes to eat lamb
with lemon and lentils.
Lubaya plays the lute
she won in a lottery
and sings lullabies
to onlookers under
a lemon tree if
she's not too lethargic.
She brings Prince William
a lavish lunch.

Princess Musidora comes from Madagascar.
She is mature, musical, and mysterious.
She eats muesli, milk shakes, and
minestrone with mint. Musidora
plays the mandolin while musing
about the moon on the marina.

For Prince William she brings
a mountain buzzard from Madagascar.

Princess Nonna comes from Narvik
in Norway. She is nice, naive, and naughty.
She likes to nosh on noodles, nuts, and
nectarines. Nonna navigates nature, looking
for nighthawks. For Prince William she
brings birds dressed in her nana's nicest
shoes and nine nifty rhino balloons.

Princess Ozeana comes from an
island at the outer edge of Oceania.
She is obliging, observant, and open-minded.
She likes oysters, okra, and oolong tea
and has even tried octopus with otter-tail soup.
Ozeana plays the oboe in the orchestra.
She brings Prince William
an olive-green frame
from Okeechobee.

Princess Piotra comes with her
pupil Petra from Poland. They are
polite, pretty, productive, and proud.
They like to eat pizza with prosciutto,
pudding with pineapples, popcorn,
and punch. Piotra promenades with
Petra picking primroses and poppies,
and attending plays. They bring Prince
William a prized plastic pet from Posen.

Princess Queena comes from Queensland.
She is quick, quirky, and sometimes quarrelsome.
She likes to eat quesadillas, quark cheese,
and quince. Queena dances the quadrille
with her friend Quasimodo when they are
not quarreling. She brings Prince William
a quiet dog called Quinn.

RENEW

ROBOT

RAGAMUFFIN

WILLIAM

Princess Renja comes from Russia.
She is radical, restless, and at times
a bit random. She likes to eat rib eye
with raisins and radish-rhubarb pie.
Renja plays the recorder in a rock 'n' roll
band with robots on roller skates. She
brings Prince William a rare radiograph.

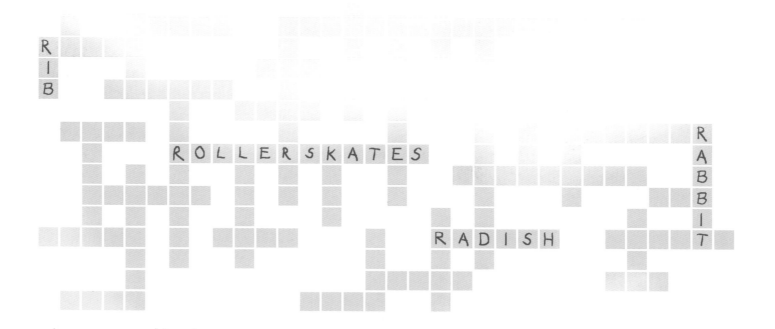

RIB

ROLLERSKATES

RADISH

RABBIT

Princess Solveig comes from Sweden.
She is shy, skillful, and sometimes silly. She likes
to eat sardines, spinach, and snickerdoodles.
She sails the seven seas singing songs and
searching for sunken shipwrecks. Solveig brings Prince
William a snowy owl, a swan, and a snow-white rabbit.

Princess Tuba
comes from Turkey.
She is timid, tactful, and tolerant.
She likes to eat trout, tomatoes with thyme,
and for dessert—tiramisu. She treks with her
teammates from Tunisia, Thailand, and Tajikistan
and wears a T-shirt that says "Take your time!"

She brings Prince William a Turkish teapot.

Princess Utina
comes from Uganda.
She is unique, useful,
and at times unruly.
She loves to eat umeboshi
plums, sea urchins, and
upside-down cake. Utina is
über-good at playing the ukulele
and puts on an unbelievable
show unless she invites her
untrained orangUtan.
She brings Prince William
an umbrella cockatoo.

Princess Victoria comes from
Venice in Veneto. She is versatile, verbose,
and sometimes vain. She likes to eat
vegetables, vanilla ice cream, and vichyssoise.
When she's not vocalizing her varied views,
she plays the violin in Verona. Victoria brings
Prince William a Venetian vizard.

Princess Wendy comes from Wrexham in Wales. She is witty, wise, and sometimes wishy-washy. She likes to eat Wiener schnitzel, waffles, and wontons. Wendy loves to walk and watch the wild waves. She brings Prince William a blue-and-white wax whale, but now she wonders if she'll give him a red one instead.

Princess Xandra
comes from Xanten.
She loves xanthic flowers
and is not at all xenophobic,
but actually quite xenophilic.
She eats xacuti masala,
xi gua lao,
and biscuits made with
xanthan gum.
She often travels
to Xiamen and
designs extraordinary
clothes with an
African xenopus
print. Xandra brings
a xylophone
for Prince William.

Princess Yoko comes from Yokohama.
She is youthful, yielding, and at times
very yappy. She eats yams and yogurt,
and drinks Yunnan tea. Yoko practices
yoga, plays with her yo-yo, and yaks
with her friends Yuri, Yukiko, and
Yutsuko. She brings Prince William
her worthY collection of Ys.

Princess Zenobia
comes from Zurich.
She is zany, zippy,
and zealous. She likes
to eat zeppelis and
zucchini with a zesty
sauce. Zenobia plays
the zither and watches
zebras when she travels
to Zimbabwe. She brings
Prince William forty
colorful pencils, from
zillabongium
to smoky topaZ.

Prince William was wowed by each
of the wondrous princesses and now
he must decide. He's waded through
his writings—weighing each gift,
each whisper and wisecrack.

His thoughts are whirling from *A* to *Z*.
Prince William is happy to take his time,
but his family insists that he decide at once.
Wish him luck!

Which of the fabulous princesses
would you choose as his best match?